D1539084

THE

OF THE WORLD

BELMONT UNIVERSITY LIBRARY
1900 E BELMONT BLVD.
NASHVILLE, TN 37212-3757

THE
WIMP
OF THE WORLD

BY

Alison Cragin Herzig

AND

Jane Lawrence Mali

Viking

VIKING
Published by the Penguin Group
Penguin Books USA Inc., 375 Hudson Street, New York, New York 10014, U.S.A.
Penguin Books Ltd, 27 Wrights Lane, London W8 5TZ, England
Penguin Books Australia Ltd, Ringwood, Victoria, Australia
Penguin Books Canada Ltd, 10 Alcorn Avenue, Toronto, Ontario, Canada M4V 3B2
Penguin Books (N.Z.) Ltd, 182–190 Wairau Road, Auckland 10, New Zealand

Penguin Books Ltd, Registered Offices: Harmondsworth, Middlesex, England

First published in 1994 by Viking, a division of Penguin Books USA Inc.

1   3   5   7   9   10   8   6   4   2

Copyright © Alison Cragin Herzig and Jane Lawrence Mali, 1994
All rights reserved

Library of Congress Cataloging-in-Publication Data
Herzig, Alison Cragin.
The wimp of the world /
by Alison Cragin Herzig and Jane Lawrence Mali.   p.   cm.
Summary: Great Aunt Dawsie springs a surprise on ten-year-old
Bridget who lives and works with her family at the Blue Moon Motel.
ISBN 0-670-85208-2
[1. Hotels, motels, etc.—Fiction.   2. Great-aunts—Fiction.]
I. Mali, Jane Lawrence.   II. Title.
PZ7.H432478Wi   1994   [Fic]—dc20   93-44487   CIP   AC

Printed in U.S.A.   Set in 13 point Caledonia
Without limiting the rights under copyright reserved above, no part of this
publication may be reproduced, stored in or introduced into a retrieval system,
or transmitted, in any form or by any means (electronic, mechanical,
photocopying, recording or otherwise), without the prior written permission
of both the copyright owner and the above publisher of this book.

184114
BELMONT UNIVERSITY LIBRARY

JuV
PZ
7
.H432478
Wi
1994

AAZ-9983

To the real Dawsie who
never found her Early
and
For Lisa, who did

—A.C.H. and J.L.M

CHAPTER

1

BRIDGET DRIBBLED THE BASKETBALL up and down the driveway of the Blue Moon Motel. The Montana sun was already hot, even for July. Her straight dirty-blonde bangs stuck to her forehead, and she could feel her cheeks getting red.

Her brothers leaned against the ice machine in the shade of the porch. All three of them were tall, with exactly the same kind of brown hair that stuck up in front.

Bridget banged at the ball as hard as she could, but it kept sputtering out. Finally it rolled away toward the VACANCY/NO VACANCY sign.

"Keep your head up, Bridger," David yelled.

"Go, go, go," Danny chanted.

Luke chewed on a long piece of grass.

Bridget dribbled the ball back. She was wearing Danny's old baseball cap. One of David's soccer jerseys hung down over her shorts.

"Maybe we should switch her to baseball or track," Danny said. "At least get her on a fitness program. Running and wind sprints."

"And push-ups," David said. "We've got to do something about her arms."

"What's wrong with my arms?" Bridget panted.

David stepped off the porch. "Look at them." He squeezed one. "Nothing but mashed potatoes. No muscle."

"Yeah," Danny agreed.

"We're just trying to get you in shape," David went on.

"You're our sister," said Luke. "We want you to be good at stuff."

"Okay," Bridget said.

"And lose those shorts," Danny said.

Bridget looked down at her knees. "But these are my favorites. Aunt Dawsie just gave them to me."

"They have dots and flowers on them." Luke pointed with his chewed piece of grass. "It's important you don't turn into a wimp."

"We already told you," David added. "You either wear full sweats or cutoffs."

"I forgot," Bridget said.

"And we'll start your fitness training tomorrow," said David.

"Yeah," Danny said. "Push-ups. First thing."

"Don't forget," said Luke. "Okay, Bridger?"

He peeled himself off the ice machine, and the three of them left her standing in the driveway. After a minute, Bridget went inside to change her shorts.

"The boys are so much bigger than me," she told her mother. "And better at everything. It's not fair. I mean, I'm only ten and they're fourteen already."

Mrs. Potter stopped frowning over a pile of bills. "I know what you mean," she said with a smile. "There are so many of them, and they take up so much room."

Bridget bounced the ball on the worn, speckled linoleum.

She stared at her mother's stomach. The new baby was going to be a boy, too. Her mother had taken a test, so they already knew that.

"And now there's going to be another one," Bridget said.

"Don't worry, sweetie. It will all work out." Mrs. Potter handed her four boxes of Kleenex. "Give these to Willow, okay?"

"I have to change my shorts," Bridget said.

"They look clean to me," her mother told her. "Besides, I'm trying to cut back on laundry. The price of water has gone sky high."

"I'll be right down." Bridget took the stairs two at a time and then stopped dead in the upstairs hallway.

An old blue crib stood against the wall right outside her room. What was it doing there? They couldn't put it in with her. Her room wasn't big enough. It wasn't even a real room. It was just a little piece at the window end of the hall that had been partitioned off with a curtain.

But where else could the baby go? The triplets needed the big bedroom, her parents had squeezed into the little one next door, and there weren't any rooms left.

Bridget sighed.

Her father had promised to build a room all for her out over the porch, with real walls and a real door. "Sometime soon," he said whenever she asked. "As soon as I have the extra cash." She planned to make a sign saying KEEP OUT. TRES-

PASSERS WILL BE VENTILATED just like the sign on her brothers' door.

But "sometime soon" never turned out to be now.

Bridget dumped the basketball into the crib.

There's always the utility room, she thought, as she stripped off her shorts. At least it would be really warm in winter, down there next to the dryer. She put her shorts back into her bureau drawer, neatly folded, like they'd never been worn, and pulled on her cutoffs.

"Bridget! Willow's waiting!" Mrs. Potter yelled from downstairs.

"Coming," Bridget yelled back. She tugged the curtain closed as far as it would go. But even so she went around to the narrow space on the other side of her bed where the boys couldn't see her, in case they came barging in the way they always did. Then she tried a push-up. She got down okay, but after that she just lay with her elbows sticking out and her face mashed into the floor.

Maybe the boys would start her on wind sprints instead. She was a pretty fast runner.

Downstairs she picked up the Kleenex boxes and carried them past the vending machines that lined the porch. Through the window of the restaurant she saw Mr. Koppel pouring coffee for the couple from Cabin 4. Their kid was standing on his chair holding a syrupy pancake in each hand. Bridget kept going. She skirted the split-rail fence around the abandoned miniature golf course and crossed the dirt road that ran beside the row of little log cabins.

All of them were exactly alike. Each had a porch with two chairs and a window box full of marigolds.

The cleaning cart was parked outside Cabin 3. Willow was on the porch shaking out a hooked rug. Her long dark braids hung down her back.

Willow was two classes ahead of Bridget at school, so Bridget had never talked to her before she came to the Blue Moon to help out for the summer. Her great-great-grandfather was a real Kiowa Indian chief, and her whole life was planned out already. She had a savings book from the bank because all the money she earned cleaning cabins and babysitting was going into a fund for college. Willow said her job at the Blue Moon was giving her a lot of good experience. But the best thing about her was that even though she was two years older, she acted as if Bridget were the same age.

Bridget stacked the Kleenex boxes on the porch

railing. "I'm sorry I'm late," she said. "I was doing push-ups."

"I've never done push-ups," Willow said. "Never even tried."

Bridget pulled the broom out of the cleaning cart.

"I've already swept," Willow said. "And we don't need to do 4 because the lady in 4 said it was too much of a mess, and the people in 11 aren't up yet. Everything else is empty. So we're done for now."

"About push-ups," Bridget said. "I can get down, but how do you get up?"

"I'll bet Aunt Dawsie does them," Willow said.

Of course, Aunt Dawsie! Aunt Dawsie would know. She could ask Aunt Dawsie anything and Aunt Dawsie wouldn't laugh. And *her* arms weren't wimpy. She had muscles. Bridget had seen them when she was splitting wood for her stove.

And she'd tell her about the crib, too. Maybe, after the baby, Aunt Dawsie would let her sleep over a lot. Even more than she did now.

"Hey, Willow, thanks." She jammed the broom back into the cart and took off for Cabin 13.

CHAPTER

2

CABIN 13 WAS THE LAST ONE on the dirt road, the
one surrounded by loblolly pines and closest to the
Clearwater River. Beside it was the dead tree with
the five messy herons' nests in it stacked one on top
of the other. And there was mint, instead of
marigolds, growing in the window box. On the
porch, next to the woodpile, was an old sofa that
swung back and forth when you sat in it. Aunt
Dawsie had lived there for three years, ever since
they had moved into the Blue Moon Motel.

"She's your great-aunt," Mr. Potter told Bridget
once. "Your grandfather's only sister. She's family.
So when we were looking for a business that all of
us could have a hand in running, she helped us buy
this place."

"We wanted to stay in Montana," Mrs. Potter added. "No where else has sky so big and yet so comforting and there's that wonderful smell when the sun warms the earth in the morning. And this place had the pine trees and the river."

"Even though it was falling apart, it was too good to pass up," Mr. Potter went on. "Dawsie said it was a once in a blue moon opportunity."

"I remember," said Bridget. "That's how the motel got named."

Mrs. Potter nodded. "Dawsie thought of it. She thinks of everything. I don't know what I would do without her."

Bridget didn't know what she would do without her, either. Cabin 13 was her favorite place.

She knocked on the door and stuck her head in. "I've got to ask you something," she called. "Really important."

"Be with you in a jiffy." Aunt Dawsie's voice floated out from the bedroom.

Her cabin was the same size as all the others. It had a bedroom in back and a living room with a pot-bellied stove and a little kitchen with a counter and three stools. But jars of bright red thimbleberry jam lined the shelf over the kitchen sink, and the cabin always smelled of pine needles and popcorn, and there was a rug with a whole deer on it in front of the pull-out sofa. Bridget turned the sofa into a bed whenever she wanted to sleep over.

"The boys say I have no muscles," Bridget shouted.

Aunt Dawsie's fishing rods leaned in the corner. And her mud boots and waders were set out on clean newspaper by the door. On the wall by the stove was a whole collection of framed black and white photographs. Bridget's favorite was the faded one of Aunt Dawsie as a little girl trail riding with her mother and father in the Rockies. Behind them wooded hills turned into mountains. Aunt Dawsie was on the biggest horse.

"Don't believe everything you hear," Aunt Dawsie called back.

Bridget checked the knitting stuff on the sofa. Aunt Dawsie was teaching her how to make a hat. After that they were going to do mittens.

Next she checked the jigsaw puzzle on the table by the window. Aunt Dawsie must have added some pieces. The edge was finished.

"But they say I need to do push-ups." Bridget

found the feet of the eagle and fit the piece in. "So you have to teach me. This afternoon. Okay?"

"It will have to be tomorrow."

"Why?" Bridget swung around.

"Because . . ." Aunt Dawsie had come out of the bedroom, but she was standing funny, sort of tilted against the wall like she was waiting for someone to take her picture. And she didn't look like Aunt Dawsie at all.

"Well." Aunt Dawsie smiled. There was lipstick on her mouth. "What do you think?" She twirled around.

Instead of jeans and a sweatshirt, she was wearing a blue flowered dress with puffy sleeves and a floaty skirt. Instead of sneakers she had on new shoes. Bright pink toenails poked out through the holes in the front.

But worst of all was her hair. Instead of long and straight and pulled back, like it should be, it was short and curling all over her head.

"Where's your hair?" Bridget asked finally. "And your regular clothes? What happened to them?"

Aunt Dawsie laughed, but it wasn't her regular laugh, either. It sounded like a giggle. "Zella

Hampel drove me to the beauty parlor right after breakfast." Aunt Dawsie patted her gray curls. "I almost chickened out, but I think I like it. And they did all my nails for free." She fanned out her hands. "I'm not sure it's me, especially the toes. Every time I look down it seems like someone else's feet, but it's fun for this once."

Aunt Dawsie's hands looked terrible. All ten of her fingernails were bright pink, too.

"But what for?"

"Come on." Aunt Dawsie giggled again. "I have something to tell your mother and father."

She clomped briskly out the front door and down the steps. On the road she tiptoed along to keep her high heels from sinking in the dirt, but she still walked fast. Bridget had to run to keep up.

They passed Willow sitting on the porch steps of Cabin 3 reading a book.

"Hey, Willow." Aunt Dawsie made her skirt swirl.

Willow looked up. Her mouth dropped open.

"Are you going to a party?" Bridget panted.

Aunt Dawsie ran her fingers along all the vending machines. The bell over the office door jangled.

Mrs. Potter stopped working. She looked even more surprised than Willow.

"Close your mouth, Dolly," said Aunt Dawsie, "and call Charlie."

"Does someone want a cabin?" Mr. Potter's head popped out of the back room.

"It's me," said Aunt Dawsie.

"She cut her hair," Bridget explained, "and they did her nails for free."

"Sure did," Aunt Dawsie went on. "Because I'm getting married!"

Married? Bridget didn't know if she'd heard right.

"Did you say married?" asked Mr. Potter.

"Married!" said Mrs. Potter.

"That's ridiculous," said Mr. Potter. "You're sixty-seven years old."

"No, I'm not. I'm sixty-eight, Charlie, and I think it's high time I tried it."

"But Aunt Dawsie," Bridget said, "can you do that?"

"You bet. And I'm going to do it up brown. A big wedding with all the trimmings. A white wedding dress *and* a veil a mile long and bridesmaids—"

"Bridesmaids!" exclaimed Mrs. Potter. "At your age?"

"Yes, bridesmaids," said Aunt Dawsie. "And a

fiddle for dancing. And a cake with those two little married folks on top . . . "

Bridget sat down on one of the office chairs. Aunt Dawsie sounded so excited, like it was the only thing she cared about. Bridget wondered whether she would remember about the push-ups.

" . . . and flowers," Aunt Dawsie was saying, "and a big potluck supper afterwards. The whole kit and kaboodle."

"But that's going to cost a fortune." Mr. Potter leaned on the reception desk. "We don't have that kind of money!"

"But I do," said Aunt Dawsie. "I've been saving my teacher's pension for a car ever since I bought the cabin, but now I won't need one."

"I don't believe what I'm hearing," said Mrs. Potter.

Bridget swallowed. "But who are you going to marry?"

Aunt Dawsie smiled at her. "You'll see," she said. "And you're going to be my maid of honor."

"But I've never even been to a wedding before."

"You'll get to wear a wonderful dress and pretty shoes and a big hat with streamers."

14

"Dolly," Bridget heard her father say, "I think Dawsie's gone round the barn."

A horn beeped in the driveway. Aunt Dawsie glanced out the window.

"There he is now," she said to Bridget.

Bridget knelt on the chair. Mr. and Mrs. Potter peered over her shoulder.

"Good heavens, Charles!" Mrs. Potter said. "It's Earl Stobbs."

Through the window Bridget saw Aunt Dawsie cross the porch. Mr. Stobbs was wearing a cowboy hat and shiny new boots. Bridget watched him take Aunt Dawsie's elbow and help her into the cab of the vending-machine refill truck as if she couldn't get in by herself. Then he folded her skirt out of the way before he closed the cab door.

The truck turned onto the highway.

Bridget sank down into the chair. She felt miserable. She didn't want Aunt Dawsie to get married. She didn't want to be in any old wedding. She'd look like the wimp of the world in a dress and a hat with streamers.

CHAPTER

3

"ARE YOU SURE Earl Stobbs isn't married already?"
Mr. Potter asked at supper. They were crowded
around the scarred wooden table in the kitchen behind the office.

"I've told you twice," Mrs. Potter said. "He was.
But she died years ago."

"Then who died at Christmas time?"

"That was his mother."

Bridget pulled at a loose thread on her cutoffs.

"Well, at least he's honest," Mr. Potter said. "He
never pads his bill."

"I know I should be happy for her," sighed Mrs.
Potter, "but it's all too sudden."

"Maybe we'll get free Cokes and candy bars
now," Danny said.

"I don't care," David said. "As long as she's back by seven-thirty. She said we could watch the baseball game with her tonight."

"And make popcorn," added Luke.

"Bridesmaids!" Mrs. Potter put down her fork. "I've just had a terrible thought. What if she asks me? I'm pregnant as a billy goat. And besides, it's been forever since I wore one of those dresses with matching shoes."

"What are matching shoes?" asked Bridget.

"They're dyed," explained her mother.

"We can't afford to take time off for all that hoopla," Mr. Potter said. "We'd have to close down for a whole weekend. And we're barely making it as it is. Half the cabins are empty since they put up that darn Big Horn Motel between us and town."

"I don't like that place." Bridget pushed her sliced carrots around her plate. "It hasn't got any trees."

"But it's computerized," her father said. "And they've got a TV dish as big as a crater right out front."

"Are we ever going to get one of those?" asked David.

17

"Maybe someday. But right now we're still paying off the reroofing and the new plumbing."

"It's one thing for Bridget to get all dolled up," said Mrs. Potter. "She'll look sweet. But it's quite another—"

Luke looked up from his mashed potatoes. His eyes narrowed. "Dolled up?"

Bridget pushed back her chair. "I don't want any dessert. So can I go now?"

"What do you mean about Bridger?" Luke asked.

Bridget didn't wait to hear. She dumped her plate in the sink and slipped out the back door.

It was her favorite time of day. The sun was all gold and still warm, but she could feel the cold coming up from the river. The little kid from Cabin 4 was running around the miniature golf course even though the faded sign said NO RUNNING ON THE GOLF COURSE. Bridget waited until his parents dragged him away.

Then she headed for the windmill hole. Her father was planning to pull the whole golf course down someday and put in a swimming pool. Weeds grew up through the gravel, and one of the little windows in the barn hole was broken. Paint was peeling off the buffalo skull. Both of the swinging doors of the Last Chance Saloon hung crooked. The sign that read SUBTRACT ONE STROKE FOR RINGING THE BELL was propped against the church.

By now her mother would have told the boys about the dress and the hat and the dyed shoes. She could almost hear them. "Yuck. Gross. Wimpy. No way."

Behind the windmill she lay facedown on the outdoor carpeting that looked like matted grass but felt like plastic. She tried a push-up. It wasn't any better than before. Only the top half of her moved. She rested for a moment and tried again. There had to be a secret.

"Hey, Bridger!" David called. "Where are you?"

Bridget scrambled to her feet.

"What are you doing back there?" asked Danny.

"Nothing."

"Is it true about the dress and the hat?" Danny asked.

"What dress?"

"You know," Luke said.

"Yeah," Danny said. "The maid-of-honor thing. Are you really going to wear it?"

"No," Bridget said.

"Because if you're going to wimp out on us, you'd better tell us now," David warned.

"I'm not."

"Have you told Aunt Dawsie?" Danny asked.

"She's not home yet."

"But it's almost time for the baseball game," David said. "This wedding stuff is ruining everything."

Luke reached up and grabbed one of the blades of the windmill even though the sign said DO NOT PLAY WITH OR STOP THE WINDMILL.

"Maybe she won't go through with it," Danny said.

Bridget remembered Aunt Dawsie's pink fingernails. "She looked really happy."

"Well, Mom and Dad aren't," said David. "So you've got to tell her as soon as she gets back that nobody wants her to get married and you're not wearing any old wedding stuff."

"Then she'll have to stick around," Danny said.

"What do you mean, stick around?" Bridget asked. "She lives here."

"Don't you know anything?" David said. "That's what getting married means. First you go away on your honeymoon for a few days and then you just go away forever and live someplace else."

"Oh," Bridget said. "Are you sure?"

"Sure, we're sure," said Luke.

"Yeah," Danny said. "Of course we're sure. So go wait on her porch, okay?"

Bridget sat in the creaky swing on Aunt Dawsie's porch watching the sun go down behind the grove of pine trees. She wished she'd brought a sweatshirt. It was cold. She piled loose pillows in her lap and pushed the swing with her toe. The herons' tree turned black against the pink and yellow sky and the sound of the river went on and on.

Bridget had just decided to go inside and sleep on the sofa bed, when she saw lights coming slowly down the dirt road. The vending-machine refill truck pulled up in front of the cabin. Earl Stobbs walked around to open Aunt Dawsie's door and help her down. Bridget heard Aunt Dawsie laugh. Then she saw Mr. Stobbs put his arms around her.

Bridget stopped swinging and hunkered down among the pillows until she could just see over the porch railing.

Aunt Dawsie's curly head tilted up, and then Bridget saw Earl Stobbs and Aunt Dawsie kiss. Right there in the road.

Bridget squeezed her eyes shut in case they were

21

going to do it again. There was a silence. Then Mr. Stobbs' slow voice said " 'Night, Dorothy. See you tomorrow, li'l darlin'."

He wasn't even whispering. The people in Cabin 12 could probably hear him, too. Then Bridget remembered that Cabin 12 was empty.

"Good night, Early dear," said Aunt Dawsie. "Sweet dreams."

Bridget wished she was anywhere except huddled in the swing on Aunt Dawsie's porch. She wished Earl Stobbs would climb back into the cab and disappear. Forever. She didn't care about the sodas and the candy bars.

Finally she heard the sound of the truck fading away down the road and Aunt Dawsie's heels on the porch steps.

"Why child, what are you doing out here?" Aunt Dawsie said. "It's so late. You must be freezing."

Bridget opened her eyes. "Hey, Aunt Dawsie."

"Come inside." Aunt Dawsie flicked on the porch lights. "I'll make us something hot."

Bridget blinked up at her. "You forgot about the game," she said.

"I'm sorry. I remembered too late." Aunt Dawsie was wearing Mr. Stobbs' jacket over her shoulders.

"But I haven't forgotten about the push-ups. And I have something wonderful to show you."

"What?"

Aunt Dawsie held out her hand. "Look at my engagement ring."

The ring had three stones, all in a row. Bridget stared at it.

"It's really pretty, I guess."

"Early gave it to me." Aunt Dawsie tilted her hand from side to side. "It was his mother's."

The three stones sparkled in the porch lights.

"I have to go now," Bridget said. She didn't know what she was going to tell the boys. But there was no way she was going to tell Aunt Dawsie not to get married. At least not tonight.

4

THE NEXT MORNING Bridget showed up after breakfast wearing her full sweats. But there was no fitness training. Even her regular ball-skills practice was canceled.

"Until further notice," Luke said.

"Until you've told her," said David.

"Yeah," added Danny.

"Boys!" Mr. Potter stuck his head out of the office door. "Stop hanging out on the porch doing nothing. Get out the lawn mower and the rakes. Looks like a hay field around the golf course."

"Aw, Dad. It takes so long," Danny said.

"What's the point?" asked Luke. "Nobody can use it. No clubs. No balls. Nothing."

"And you promised you were going to buy one of those tractor mowers," David reminded him. "With a grass bag on the back."

"You think money grows on trees? Bridget, you're supposed to help Mr. Koppel in the restaurant and then clean with Willow." The door of the office slammed shut.

"Dad looks like he slept on his face," David said.

"Mr. Koppel hates it when I help," Bridget said. "He says I spill coffee in the saucers."

"At least he gets paid," David told her.

"So does Willow," said Bridget.

"I wish we did," Danny grumbled. "I hate it when Dad says we're all in this together."

"And that bit about 'I don't get paid. Your mother doesn't get paid. You don't get paid,'" David mimicked. " 'We're family.' "

"We're slaves," said Luke.

"You remember that place we heard about?" David asked. "Where you could see the world's biggest ball of string? Why don't we make a bigger one? And charge admission."

"Yeah," agreed Danny. "How hard could it be?"

"Hard," said Luke.

"Boys!" Mr. Potter bellowed through the window. "Get hopping!"

"I'll mow," Luke said. "You two rake."

"What's to help?" Mr. Koppel asked when Bridget showed up. "Do you see anyone yelling for service?"

The tables were empty.

"Those big eaters from Nebraska in 3 cleared out early this morning." Mr. Koppel ran a cloth over the clean counter. "There's no one left except that young couple in Cabin 11 who don't eat breakfast and that family in 4 with the little kid who never stops running. That's it. And I made corn bread. Special."

"I could take a piece to Willow."

"Why not," said Mr. Koppel. "It'll be hard as a rock by noon. And take a piece to your Aunt Dawsie. I hear she's getting hitched."

"Maybe," Bridget said.

She rolled the cleaning cart to Cabin 3. Willow was nowhere around. After awhile Bridget put the corn bread on the windowsill in the little kitchen and started emptying the wastepaper baskets and stripping the beds. Wet towels littered the bathroom floor, and dirty glasses filled the sink. Bridget hoped Willow would come soon. Cleaning was more fun with two.

She was about to start on the bathroom when she heard Willow bang through the screen door.

"Sorry, sorry, sorry," she said. "I was down at the river. Aunt Dawsie was trying to teach me how to fish again. Isn't it great about her and Earl Stobbs and the big wedding? It's so romantic!"

"There's corn bread on the windowsill," Bridget said. "I've got to get the tub cleaner."

Willow followed her outside. "And she asked me to be a bridesmaid. I'm going to wear a dress with a big skirt and a hat with—"

"Willow, look! That kid from 4 just took our toilet brush right out of the cart. And he doesn't have any pants on!"

"Hey, you! We need that!" Willow shouted.

The little kid took off down the road in his red sneakers and T-shirt.

His mother came charging out of the next cabin. She chased after him in her bare feet, waving a pair of underpants and yelling and trying to button up her blue jeans all at the same time.

"Darn it!" Willow started down the steps.

"I'll get him," Bridget said.

"Frankie! Come here this minute! Franklin!" The mother stopped to brush something off the bottom of one foot.

Frankie disappeared into the grove of pine trees behind Aunt Dawsie's cabin. His mother hobbled after him. Bridget tore past her as if the woman were standing still. She felt like a racer. Her legs churned. If only the boys were there to see.

When she broke through the trees, the kid was crouched on the bank of the river, bashing at the water with the brush. His bare bottom shone in the sun.

"Hey, give that back!" Bridget shouted at him.

Frankie gave her one quick look and plunged into the shallow water.

"Wait!" Bridget yelled.

Somewhere behind her she heard faint shouts, like bird calls. "Come back," she yelled. "It's okay. All I want is the brush."

But Frankie kept splashing and bashing downstream.

Bridget trailed him along the bank. There was no point in getting her sweats all wet. Anyway, the water was freezing. Any minute he'd give up and come out.

Then suddenly she remembered the deep swimming hole.

She scrambled down the bank. The water filled her sneakers and dragged at her sweats. Frankie had almost reached the bend in the river. The swimming hole was right ahead of him!

Bridget tried to run, but she kept slipping and sliding on the rocks. She'd never reach him in time.

Then she saw Aunt Dawsie on the opposite bank in her high bib waders, carrying her fishing rod.

Frankie saw her, too. He spun around. Bridget was almost on him. Frankie gave a little shriek and tried to duck past her.

Bridget grabbed his T-shirt. "Got you," she said.

"Hang on!" Aunt Dawsie plowed through the water toward them. "Take my rod." She tucked Frankie, wiggling and kicking, under her arm. He bashed at her with the toilet brush.

Bridget waded to shore. A moment later Aunt Dawsie dumped Frankie on the bank beside her.

"Sit on him," she said. "He's as slippery as a fish."

"Oh, Frankie!" His mother came crashing through the thimbleberry bushes. She scooped him up in her arms and began to kiss his wet face. "Never, never do that again."

"I can swim," said Frankie.

"No you can't," his mother said. "Thank you, thank you," she said to Aunt Dawsie between kisses. "How can I ever thank you enough?"

"Wasn't me. It was Bridget who landed him. But I'd get him home if I were you," Aunt Dawsie added. "He looks a little blue."

Frankie pointed the toilet brush at Bridget. "She wants my brush."

"It's not your brush," Bridget said.

"Give it back, darling," the mother said.

"My brush, my brush," Frankie chanted.

"Oh, dear . . ." His mother shrugged. "I'll get it back," she mouthed, "when he takes his nap."

"No nap! No nap!" screamed Frankie, as his mother carried him off.

"Well," said Aunt Dawsie. "I guess that's enough fishing for today." She began to unbuckle her waders. Underneath she was wearing long under-wear. The blue-and-white striped ones. Bridget had seen them a million times hanging from the clothesline behind Cabin 13.

Suddenly she felt like crying.

Aunt Dawsie put an arm around her. "Are you okay?"

"Yes," Bridget said. Her sweats were wet and cold and heavy. "But what would have happened if you hadn't been here? He probably would have drowned in the pool."

"You caught him. I only helped get him ashore. We're a good team."

"Nothing's good," Bridget burst out. "Everything's horrible." She hugged her wet knees. "Dad's mad. The cabins are pretty near empty. Everyone's at that other motel. And now your cabin will be empty, too, and I'll have no place to go. And I can't do push-ups and Mom's having another boy and they'll probably put him in my room and then I'll really have nowhere . . ." Bridget was crying now. "So I'm sorry about Mr. Stobbs," she hiccupped. "But don't you see? You can't get married. You can't go away."

"Good heck," Aunt Dawsie said. "This is a fine how-do-you-do." She stroked Bridget's back and stared across the river. After awhile Bridget wiped her eyes with the sleeve of her sweatshirt.

"I need some popcorn," Aunt Dawsie said at last.

"Popcorn? In the morning?"

"Yes, popcorn. And lemonade with lots of ice and a sprig of mint. Food helps me think. And it looks like I have some fast thinking to do."

CHAPTER

5

THE POPCORN WAS ALL GONE. There was nothing but a few unpopped kernels at the bottom of the bowl. Aunt Dawsie sighed. Then she licked her fingers and picked up the phone on her kitchen counter.

"Are you calling Earl Stobbs?" Bridget asked.

Aunt Dawsie put her hand over the mouthpiece. "No. I'm calling Zella Hampel. We need a ride."

"But what about the wedding?"

"First things first," Aunt Dawsie said. "Go change out of those wet clothes. And tell your mom and dad you'll be gone until lunch."

When Bridget got back to Cabin 13 in her flowered shorts, Zella Hampel's old blue station wagon was parked out front. Bridget climbed into the back-seat. "Where are we going?"

"On a fact-finding tour," Aunt Dawsie said. She was wearing the puffy-sleeved dress from yesterday.

Zella Hampel gunned the car down the dirt road and out onto the highway.

"You might want to slow down, Zella," Aunt Dawsie suggested. Bridget leaned her arms on the back of the front seat. Zella was even older than Aunt Dawsie, and so short she had to sit on a pillow to see over the steering wheel.

"Zella, are you weaving or is it my imagination?" Aunt Dawsie asked a little later.

"I'm still on my side of the white line." Zella bumped the car over a metal cattle guard.

"There," Aunt Dawsie said. "It's just past that Taco Bell."

"I can still see, Dawsie," Zella said. She jammed on the brakes and lurched over the curb into the driveway of the new Big Horn Motel.

"What are we doing here?" Bridget asked.

"Snooping," Aunt Dawsie said.

The motel was two stories high and all white, with a wagon-wheel fence. In front a huge television dish took up most of the patch of lawn. Next to it was a sign like a movie theater's. A man on a ladder was changing the letters. WELCOME SUMMER FOLKS! SEE OUR OVERSIZED ROOMS! Bridget read, and under that, CONGRATULATIONS HORACE AND MARGAR. What kind of a name was Margar? she wondered.

"How long will you be?" Zella asked. "I want to get my hair straightened."

"Straightened?" Aunt Dawsie said. "You just had it curled."

"I can't be a bridesmaid with it all frizzy like this."

Bridget saw the man add an E and a T to the sign. She wondered if Horace and Margaret had just gotten married.

"Then come back when you're through." Aunt Dawsie climbed out of the car. "We'll be waiting outside."

Bridget followed her into the motel. The doors opened automatically, like the ones at the supermarket. "Now, Bridget," Aunt Dawsie said in a low voice, "keep your eyes peeled."

Bridget looked around. There were big green plants in pots on either side of the reception desk. "For what?" she asked.

"For something we have and they don't. For something that would make people want to come to the Blue Moon rather than here."

"Oh," Bridget said.

"Exactly!" Aunt Dawsie squeezed her shoulder and winked.

The man behind the desk looked up as Aunt Dawsie marched toward him. She rang the bell anyway.

"Can I help you?" the man said politely. Bridget noticed that he was wearing an orange jacket and a string tie with a silver bucking-bronco clasp.

"I certainly hope so," said Aunt Dawsie. "I'm planning a very large function in the near future. With a great many guests."

"A banquet? Or will they be staying overnight?" the man asked. The pin on his jacket said Manager.

"Possibly both," said Aunt Dawsie. "Depending on how oversized your oversized rooms are."

"And how many did you say would be in your party?" the manager asked.

"How many?" Aunt Dawsie looked at Bridget. "How many would you say, Bridget?"

"Lots," said Bridget. "Pretty near a hundred."

"Very good." The manager smiled and rubbed his hands together. "Just let me get someone to take over the desk and I'll show you around myself."

"We have a postcard rack," Bridget said to Aunt Dawsie.

"You're right. Good thinking."

"But I don't think it's enough," Bridget said.

When the manager came back, he was carrying a ring of keys. "Right this way, ladies," he said. "We can start with the pool."

The pool was in the middle of the motel. Rows of balconies looked down on it and all around were deck chairs and tubs of flowers. Bridget counted fifteen people sunning themselves. She had never seen water so blue.

"But why does it smell funny?" she asked.

"That's chlorine, of course," said the manager. "For the health of our guests. And heated right through to October. Then we put it to bed for the winter."

"The river smells nice all year round," Bridget whispered to Aunt Dawsie. "And you can fish in it."

"Do you think that's enough?"

"No," said Bridget. "They have a diving board. We just have tubing."

On the second-floor balcony the manager unlocked a door. "This is one of our beautiful standard doubles," he said, "and we can roll in a child's bed at no extra charge."

A thick brown rug covered the whole floor. The bedspread was printed with rodeo scenes and fringed at the bottom. Bridget pictured the faded blue spreads and hooked rugs in the cabins at home.

Aunt Dawsie opened one of the cabinets in the kitchenette. "Plastic dishes," she said. "Hmm."

"Most of our guests don't cook," the manager said. "They have breakfast by the pool in our Hungry Horse Café. Other meals are always available in our Gold Dust Lounge or, for more elegant dining, in the Ponderosa Room."

Bridget thought about Mr. Koppel and his corn bread. She stared at the television set across from the bed. It had millions of buttons. On top was a sign. FIRST RUN MOVIES AVAILABLE TWENTY-FOUR HOURS A DAY ON CHANNEL 31. The only cabin with TV at the Blue Moon was Aunt Dawsie's.

"There are no woodstoves," she whispered.

"You're right. It's a pity," said Aunt Dawsie.

The manager led them out onto the balcony and

unlocked another door. He showed them through a suite with two bedrooms and two white-tiled bathrooms and three television sets. The boys would love this place, Bridget thought.

"And of course we have room service at a nominal fee," the manager was saying, "and you can get your clothes cleaned and your shoes shined while you sleep."

"No vending machines," whispered Bridget.

"Don't tell Early."

A lady in an orange uniform pushed a cleaning cart along the balcony. Bridget wondered what there was to clean. Everything looked brand new. She leaned over the railing and stared down at the pool. It was a really nice pool. Bridget remembered Frankie running down the dirt road toward the river and— Then she remembered something else.

"That's everything, except for the conference rooms," the manager said, "and our video-game arcade."

"Bridget, should we see the video-game arcade?"

"No," Bridget said. "We've found all the facts we need."

"We have?"

"Yes." Bridget wanted to jump up and down. But

she couldn't with the manager standing right there. Instead she winked.

Aunt Dawsie smiled. "There's just one more thing," she said to the manager. "I presume you take animals. One of my guests has a pet pig."

"A pig?" The manager looked horrified.

"Sure does. A little black one," Aunt Dawsie said. "She never travels without it."

"I'm sorry." The manager took a step back. "A pig is out of the question."

"Actually, it's sort of pinkish-black," Bridget said.

"And its name is Pookie Pig," said Aunt Dawsie.

"And it's a really good pig," Bridget went on. "It only goes, you know, outdoors."

"No pig!" the manager said firmly.

"How disappointing," Aunt Dawsie told him. "I'm afraid we've been wasting our time. Come on, Bridget. I reckon we'll have to look elsewhere."

"There's the Blue Moon Motel down the road," Bridget said. "That's nice."

"Funny," Aunt Dawsie said. "I've never been there."

Bridget held her breath to keep from laughing.

"We can show ourselves out," Aunt Dawsie told the manager.

Bridget led the way down the stairs and through the lobby. "Miniature golf!" she shouted as soon as the automatic doors closed behind them. "They don't have golf!"

"Golf?" Aunt Dawsie hesitated.

"I know the course is sort of wrecked," Bridget said. "But we could fix it up."

Aunt Dawsie stared at her for a moment. "It just might work," she said.

A horn tooted. The blue station wagon careened into the driveway. Zella Hampel stuck her head out the window.

"They can't fix my hair," she said. "I'll have to hide it under my hat."

Aunt Dawsie laughed. "Never mind that, Zella. Bridget and I have more important things to fix." She climbed into the backseat next to Bridget. Didn't I tell you we made a good team?" she said on the way home. "Didn't I?"

CHAPTER

6

"THIS BETTER COVER THE COST of all that paint," Mr. Potter said two weeks later. "Not to mention the hardware and the brushes and—"

"Now, Charlie, you've got to admit it's beautiful," Mrs. Potter interrupted. "So pretty and colorful. Makes the whole place look brand new."

The windmill had been freshly painted a gaudy green. The Last Chance Saloon was now bright blue with white trim and the yellow buckboard seat rested between shiny black wagon wheels. A coat of gold glitter nail polish covered each of the cash register keys; the wishing well had a pink bucket; the reflector on the railroad crossing shone like a stop light; and Humpty Dumpty had been set back on his orange brick wall. The broken window in the allred barn had been fixed, and the church and the steer skull gleamed glossy white in the early moring sun. The weeds in the gravel pathways were gone.

"It wasn't so easy to fix the saloon doors," David said. "But I did it."

"I like the giant pinball machine best," said Mrs. Potter.

"I like the rattlesnake, because the ball has to go round and round," said Bridget.

"Who put that black thing on the skull?" asked Mr. Potter.

"I did," said Aunt Dawsie. "And it's not a thing, Charlie. It's a mustache."

"My favorite is the six-foot rabbit," said Willow. "I like his red vest and his polka-dotted tie."

"Let's hit a few balls." David picked a new putter from the rebuilt rack.

"Yeah. Try it out," said Danny.

"Paint's still wet," Luke said.

"Besides, we're not done yet," added Aunt Dawsie. She turned to Bridget and Willow. "Top-level strategy session. On the double. Cabin 13."

After supper that night everyone trooped outside to look at the golf course again. Aunt Dawsie brought a cup of tea from her cabin, and even Mr. Koppel walked the gravel pathways with a dish towel tucked into his belt.

"That big billboard out by the flagpole with GOLF on it is really eye catching," said Mrs. Potter.

"That was Aunt Dawsie's idea," said Bridget.

"Well, where are all these golfers?" Mr. Potter wanted to know. "How many fliers did you say you put up downtown?"

"We only made nine," Bridget said. "First we had to think of the strategy and all the words and it was a lot of writing for me and Willow. But we put one up in the window of the Safeway and the Crimp and Primp Hairdressers and the Army/Navy Store and the Plum Dandy Dress Shop on Higgins Street and some other places and then Zella drove us home. And there's still this last one for the office."

"Let me see." Mr. Potter read the words out loud.

Attention Sports Fans!!!
Announcing the Grand Opening of the
All New, Totally Renovated, Colorful,
Challenging,
Jim-Dandy, World-Class

BLUE MOON MOTEL MINIATURE GOLF
COURSE.
Only One of Its Kind in the Area!
Join the Fastest Growing Sport in the Whole
U.S. of A.!
Eighteen Holes for the Price of Nine.
Adults $3.50   Seniors $2.50   Kids $1.00
Rent a Cabin!   Play for Free!

"Willow thought of 'challenging,'" Bridget explained, "and Aunt Dawsie thought of 'jim-dandy,' and I thought of the 'only one of its kind' part, because it is."

"There's not a word about food," said Mr. Koppel.

"We were going to add that and tubing on the river and our postcard rack and the wood-burning stoves, but there wasn't room," Bridget said.

"It can't be the fastest growing sport," said David. "I mean what about basketball?"

"Yeah," said Danny.

"It is so," insisted Bridget. "Aunt Dawsie heard it on a sports wrap-up program."

"It's true," said Luke.

Aunt Dawsie sipped her tea. "I'm glad the bell in

the church still works." There was a smudge of yellow paint on the back of her hand.

"Yoo hoo!" A woman in shorts and sandals appeared around the side of the motel. "Can someone here help us? There's no one in the office."

"Good heavens! I'll be right with you," said Mrs. Potter.

"My, this sure is a nice golf course. My husband saw your sign at the gas station."

"Shirley, did you find anyone?" A man in loafers and high black socks came up behind her. "Do they have a vacancy?"

"Cabin 7 is available," said Mrs. Potter, "or Cabin 12, if you'd prefer to be closer to the river."

"Look at this course, Clint," the woman said. "If we hurry we can get in a couple of rounds before dark."

"Come back to the office," said Mrs. Potter. "It won't take a minute to get you all checked in."

"The restaurant's still open, if you're hungry," offered Mr. Koppel.

"David! Danny! See if they need help with their bags," said Mr. Potter. "And lay a fire in the stove. It can get chilly at nights."

"Shall I tell them they can leave their shoes outside the door and I'll polish them?" Bridget whispered to Aunt Dawsie. "Like they do at the Big Horn?"

"The racoons would get them," Aunt Dawsie said.

"Dad?" Luke said.

"What?"

"Can the golf course be a pay job?"

"Pay? For what?"

"To keep the course from getting beat up again. Make sure the clubs get returned. Find lost balls. Collect the money. You know, management. David, Danny, and me."

"If it goes . . ." Mr. Potter hesitated. "Well, then, I might be able to work something out."

"Hey, what about me?" Bridget tugged at Luke's sleeve. "It was my idea."

Luke eyed her for a moment. Then he nodded. "When you're older," he said. "But you have to be at least twelve."

Before she went upstairs to bed Bridget called Willow to tell her that the signs were already working.

"That's great!" said Willow.

"Even Dad's happy," Bridget said.

Her father was whistling in the kitchen and, better than that, she hadn't seen Earl Stobbs in days. He'd disappeared and Aunt Dawsie didn't seem to care.

But when she reached the top of the stairs, she found that someone had put stacks of baby clothes in the old blue crib in the hall outside her room.

Bridget stared at them. Then she went into her room and rested her elbows on the windowsill. She gazed out at the golf course. The new people were just putting their clubs away.

"You almost beat me this time, honey," she heard Shirley say. Clint didn't answer.

The last of the sunset reflected in the new window of the miniature red barn. If only the barn were a little bigger, she thought, just big enough to fit my bed. I wouldn't need a chair or anything. And I wouldn't even care if golf balls came through.

CHAPTER

7

"WE'VE NEVER HAD TO DO seven cabins in a day before," Bridget said as she helped push the cleaning cart piled high with dirty towels and sheets back toward the motel.

Cars lined the dirt road. Way at the far end she could see Zella's blue station wagon parked in front of Cabin 13.

"Look at all those people waiting to play golf," Willow said. "And it's such a boring game."

Bridget glanced over. It had only been a week, but there were people on the course and more people waiting. The boys were manning the ticket table by the gate. Sometimes they even ate their supper out there. Besides tickets, they'd made T-shirts to sell, with THE BLUE MOON GOLF COURSE stenciled on the front. All they did was golf-course management now. They never mentioned her ball skills or fitness training anymore.

"I know," she said. "But Dad's even talking about putting up lights someday, so people can play night golf."

"Hey, Willow," Danny yelled. "Want a putting lesson later? Only fifty cents."

"Forget it," Willow said. "You'd have to pay me to play."

"Then bring me a Coke on your way back, Bridget."

"Yeah, me too. This is hot work," David added.

"Make that three," said Luke.

"Get them yourself," Willow said.

"They'll be mad," Bridget whispered.

"That's their tough." Willow pushed the cart into the utility room.

Mrs. Potter was folding clean sheets on the table against the wall. "Just leave the cart," she said. "That's enough work for one day. And Willow, don't forget it's Friday, payday. And your mother called. She can't pick you up until late this afternoon."

Bridget followed Willow into the office and watched her open the envelope and count the money. Then she stuck the bills between the pages of her little blue bankbook. Bridget wondered what it would feel like to carry a book like that around in her back pocket the way Willow always did, and whether the boys would get bankbooks now, too.

"Want to go to Aunt Dawsie's for some mint lemonade?" she asked.

"Sure. And then maybe we could go tubing, if I could borrow a pair of cutoffs. We could walk to Split Rock or get Zella to drop us off further up, at the bridge."

"She comes every day to play golf," Bridget said.

"I know," said Willow. "Ever since she scored that hole in one."

But when they pushed open the door to Cabin 13, Zella wasn't wearing her golfing skirt. She was standing on the coffee table in a long pink dress, turning slowly like a figure on a music box. Aunt Dawsie knelt on the rug in her jeans. Her mouth was full of pins.

"Are you sure you made it short enough, Daws?" Zella was saying. "I want my ankles to show. They're my best feature."

"Oh, Zella!" Willow exclaimed. "Is that your bridesmaid's dress? It's so beautiful!"

"But I thought Earl Stobbs was gone," Bridget said.

Aunt Dawsie sat back on her heels and took the pins out of her mouth. "He was, at a vending-machine convention, but he's back now. I'm all done, Zella. You can get out of the dress now."

"I can't wait," said Willow. "Where's mine? Can I try it on?"

Aunt Dawsie glanced at Bridget. "The others haven't come yet. Besides, I've done enough wedding stuff for today."

"Where's my knitting?" Bridget asked.

"In the chair by the stove," Aunt Dawsie told her.

Bridget sat down and pushed the stitches back and forth on the needle.

"Oh, lawdy!" Zella scrambled off the table. "Earl's here! I don't want him to see me. I want it to be a surprise." She gathered up her skirts and rustled into the bedroom.

Bridget jabbed the point of the needle through the next stitch of her knitting. Zella looked like the wimp of the world in that dress. It was exactly the color of bubble gum after it was chewed.

Earl Stobbs took off his hat as he came through the door. "Hey, where's my li'l darlin'?" he asked.

"Hey, yourself." Aunt Dawsie's cheeks had turned a sudden red.

Earl kissed her fingers. "I shouldn't even have stopped, but I couldn't wait to see you."

"Have you got time for a mint lemonade?" Aunt Dawsie asked.

Earl shook his head. "I've got to check in at the warehouse, but I'll be back to take you out for supper."

Bridget was sick of knitting. She stuffed the hat and the ball of wool into the crack between the cushion and the arm of the chair.

"Is that up the river, past the bridge?" Willow asked. "Bridget and I want to go tubing."

"Willow." Bridget glared at her. "I thought we were going to walk."

"I'd be honored to give you gals a lift," Earl said, "as far as you want to go."

"We have to find cutoffs for you and pump up the tubes and everything, Willow," said Bridget. "We won't be ready for ages."

"I'll wait for you out in front of the office," Earl said.

When they rolled the tubes past the vending machines, Earl was standing at the back of his truck with the doors open. He bounced the tubes in on top of the cases of soda.

Bridget let Willow climb into the cab first.

"I love riding in trucks," Willow said. "You're so high up, you look down right through peoples' sunroofs."

"I know." Earl gave a little laugh. "I never told anybody before, but it makes me feel like a rajah on an elephant."

Bridget stared out the window at the tops of cars and dry fields and sagebrush. In the distance she could see the green of the trees that lined the river, and beyond them the gray-blue of the mountains.

"I'm wondering if you could give me some help, Bridget," Earl said after a moment. "I bought your Aunt Dorothy a present on my trip, something I found in a mall in Red Lodge, but I'm not so sure about it. And I reckon you know her better than anyone."

"What is it?" Willow asked.

"We're almost at the bridge," Bridget said.

"I'll get it out as soon as I pull over," Earl said.

"There's a place where fishermen park just ahead," Willow told him.

Bridget dribbled her tube two-handed on the

gravel turnout while Earl went back to the cab for the thing he'd bought.

"It's for her porch," he said, unwrapping layers of newspaper.

Aunt Dawsie's porch was just the way she liked it, Bridget thought. It didn't need anything else.

Two pieces of metal fell out of the paper, a solid square and a sort of a wishbone attached by fish line to a metal bar.

"It's a wind chime," Earl explained, holding it up by the bar. "I know it doesn't look like much at first, but I thought it made a nice sound."

"I love wind chimes," Willow said. "Don't you, Bridget?"

Bridget stared at it. The square began to turn, and slowly, slowly the wishbone swung around, until the two metal pieces touched and pinged and the wishbone was sent back the other way. Earl blew on it gently. The two pieces touched again.

"You see," he said to Bridget, "I thought this was pretty near the sound that stars might make if they bumped into each other."

Bridget pictured sitting in the swinging sofa on the porch after dark with the sound of the river running in the background and every now and then the ping of little stars bumping.

"It's . . . it's good," she said finally. "She'll like it."

"Do you think?"

"Yes. Really."

Earl grinned all over his face. "That's just what I needed to hear. Then I'll give it to her soon as I get back."

A narrow trail cut down the steep bank to the Clark Fork. Earl watched them launch the tubes into the river. Tubing was like riding in a rocking armchair, Bridget thought, except your bottom and feet were in the water. She was always surprised at how cold the water was and how hot the rubber tube stayed in the sun.

The current spun her around. Earl stood on the bank, looking after them. The tube swung around again. Just before she reached the bend in the river Bridget raised a hand and waved. Earl whipped off his hat and swung it wildly over his head.

"Bridget!" Willow shouted. "Rocks ahead. Butts up!"

CHAPTER

8

AFTER WILLOW LEFT, Bridget went to the utility room to put the wet cutoffs into the dryer. Mrs. Potter looked up from stacking sheets.

"I've been here all afternoon, and I'd still be folding if Dawsie hadn't helped," she said. "But I guess that's the price of success."

"What are you going to do if Dad puts in lights?" Bridget asked.

Her mother smiled. "Go to bed and pull the covers over my head. By the way, Dawsie wants to see you."

"Where are the boys?"

"Glued to their ticket table, where else?"

Bridget went out the front so they wouldn't see her. Mr. Koppel was outside the restaurant, fanning himself with a menu. "Three pans of corn bread gone like that." He snapped his fingers. "I'd be dead if'n I had the time to sit down."

Bridget counted the cars along the dirt road. There were eight of them. She remembered when the road used to be almost empty. Now it looked more like a parking lot.

Aunt Dawsie was standing on the far side of her cabin, staring at something through her binoculars.

"What are you looking at?" Bridget asked.

"The nests. I think the last of the baby herons have flown. Here. Have a look."

Through the binoculars the nests seemed like messy piles of twigs that had just happened to land in a tree.

"Why doesn't the wind blow them down?" Bridget asked.

"Must be more to it than meets the eye, or else they're held together by wishful thinking."

"I don't see any little heads sticking up."

"Well, that's it for this year then, but they'll be back. Maybe not the same herons—different herons using the same old nests. Sort of like the Clearwater. Same old river, different water."

Bridget handed the binoculars back.

"I have a confession to make," Aunt Dawsie went on. "Willow's dress *is* here. And so is yours. But I wanted us to see yours first—just you and me."

"Isn't it the same as Zella's?"

Aunt Dawsie shook her head. "Willow's is, but the bride and the maid of honor should look different from everybody else."

The dress was hanging in Aunt Dawsie's closet. It wasn't pink at all. It was white, but so covered with little sprigs of flowers that the white hardly showed. There was a wide pink ribbon sash and a long skirt with a ruffle of extra material at the bottom.

Aunt Dawsie laid it on her bed and stepped back.

The puffy sleeves were completely stuffed with tissue paper, and the dress was so new that tags were still hanging from it.

"There's a hat and shoes too, but I thought you'd like to decide about the dress first," Aunt Dawsie said.

"How do you know it's going to fit?" Bridget asked.

"I don't," said Aunt Dawsie. "I guess you'll have to try it on."

"And then will you show me about push-ups?"

"Good heck! I almost forgot. I asked around and

here's the thing: free weights. They're better for upper-body strength and upper-body strength isn't a bad thing to have."

"Free weights?" Bridget repeated.

"I know," Aunt Dawsie said. "I thought it meant getting something for nothing, too, but all it means is you hold them in your hands, like miniature barbells. It's good for people of all ages." Aunt Dawsie sighed. "I wish I had more time before the wedding. We could do them together."

Bridget sat down on the bed. "I wish you did too. And I wish I didn't have to go back to school right after."

The wedding was only two weeks and two days away.

The summer was almost over, Bridget thought, and she hadn't noticed. Everything was almost over. "And then you'll go away like the boys said. Right?"

"Yes, but not very far. Earl's house is just down the highway on the other side of town. You can come visit any time you want."

"Does it have the river?"

"No. That makes me a little sad. But I know where to find it."

Bridget shifted on the bed. The dress rustled. "Do

I have to try it on with all the paper in it?" she asked.

Aunt Dawsie laughed. "Everyone would hear you coming, that's for sure."

The dress felt funny. It was so light Bridget could hardly tell she was in it, but when she turned, the skirt swirled around her sneakers.

"There's a mirror on the closet door," Aunt Dawsie reminded her.

Bridget blinked at the girl in the mirror. A princess in a baseball cap blinked back.

"Now, about the hat and shoes, you don't have to wear them. No, sirree. You can wear that cap instead." Aunt Dawsie put her hand on Bridget's shoulder. Bridget could see all of her in the mirror, too. "Actually, you don't have to wear the dress either. You can wear anything you want."

"I want to see the shoes," Bridget said.

She was in her room behind the curtain, trying on the hat, shoes, and dress again before supper, when she heard the boys coming up the stairs.

"Hey, Bridger." It was David.

Bridget didn't answer. She hoped they'd think she was out somewhere.

"There she is. I can see her through the curtain," Danny said.

He pulled the curtain back, and the three of them crowded in.

Bridget wished for the millionth time that she had a door so at least they'd have to knock.

"We were looking for you," Danny announced. "And what's that stuff you've got on?"

"And that thing on your head?" David asked.

It was amazing how well she could see them, Bridget discovered, through the straw brim of her hat.

"They're my maid-of-honor clothes."

"It's flowered. It's got a pink belt," Luke said. "It's a No."

"Boys," Mr. Potter called from downstairs. "Hurry and wash up. It's time for supper."

"You want to see my shoes?" Bridget asked.

"I knew this would happen," David said. "The moment we turned our backs."

"Her fitness training's gone down the tubes," Danny agreed. "I hope we haven't lost too much ground."

"We've got to get her on track again," David

went on. "Find time early in the morning before we get too tied up with our business."

"Double session, starting tomorrow," Luke said. "In your full sweats."

Bridget took a step toward them. Her whole room smelled of their sneakers. "I'm not doing that anymore," she said. "I'm doing free weights instead."

"Free weights? How does she know about them?" David asked.

"Who told her?" demanded Luke.

"Don't look at me," Danny said.

"For upper-body strength," Bridget added.

"Bridget! Boys! Supper!" yelled Mr. Potter.

"Get out of my room," Bridget said. "I have to change into my shorts. My flowered ones."

CHAPTER

9

THE END OF THE DIRT ROAD was covered with hay to keep the dust down.

Step. Pause. Step. Pause. The hay whispered under Bridget's feet. She could smell the mint Aunt Dawsie had tucked into her bouquet of flowers.

It was hard to walk slowly all by yourself, she thought, with strangers from the cabins and the Saturday golfers and everybody's friends watching you. She caught a glimpse of her father and her brothers in shirts with collars. Comb lines still showed in their wet hair.

The little band of fiddlers struck up "Here Comes the Bride" all over again. At the end of the hay path she could see her mother and Zella and Willow, pink against the green pine trees, and on the other side of the minister, Earl standing all alone.

Finally she was there. Earl smiled at her, but his blue eyes stared over her shoulder. Bridget turned around to see Aunt Dawsie come floating toward them.

A cloud of white veiling fell past her shoulders, and the top of her old-fashioned white dress was all lace up to her chin, with long sleeves that ended in points embroidered with more lace, and a skirt that trailed behind her forever.

"It was my mother's wedding dress," Aunt Dawsie had told her back at the cabin. "I don't know why, but I saved it all these years."

Bridget couldn't see them, but she knew there were a hundred little white buttons going all down the back.

The fiddlers sawed to a stop. In the silence Bridget could hear the running of the river from beyond the trees.

"Hey," Earl whispered and took Aunt Dawsie's hand.

"Hey yourself," said Aunt Dawsie.

The minister cleared his throat. "Dearly beloved . . ." he began. He had a lot to say. Bridget stood as still as she could, waiting. She was listening for Aunt Dawsie to say, "I will."

Someone sniffed. It was Mrs. Potter. The brim of her hat fluttered. She was smiling and crying at the same time.

"I will, I sure will," Earl said.

"I will, too," Aunt Dawsie said.

"Who giveth this woman to be married to this man?" the minister asked.

Bridget hoped her voice would come out okay. "I do," she said.

It sounded too loud, but no one seemed to mind.

After that everything began to go very fast. Aunt Dawsie handed Bridget her bouquet to hold, and then she and Earl gave each other rings, and then the minister said, "Let us now have the blessing," and Willow stepped forward.

First she spoke in Kiowa, and then she said, "This is the People's Wedding Blessing," and repeated it all again in English.

"And now for you there is no rain,
    for one of you is shelter to the other.
And now for you there is no burning sun . . .
And now for you there is no hard or bad . . ."

She wasn't reading from a piece of paper or anything. She had it all memorized.

"Go now to your dwelling to enter into the days of your life together . . ." Willow said.

There was a loud sniff from Mrs. Potter.

"And may your days be good and long upon the earth," Willow finished.

And then everyone was hugging everyone, and Bridget gave Aunt Dawsie back her flowers, and Earl kissed Aunt Dawsie, and they were married to each other.

"Now listen up, friends," Earl said. "The party's over at the golf course. Food and dancing and soda. We're going to have a dilly of a time."

"And free golf for everyone!" Mr. Potter shouted.

"And a wedding cake," Aunt Dawsie added. "Chocolate with vanilla icing."

In the distance the bell on the miniature church in the golf course began to clang.

Aunt Dawsie laughed. "That's Mr. Koppel, right on cue." She swooped up her long skirt and draped it over her arm. "Come on, Bridget! I'm starving!"

It was getting dark. Zella had finally come off the

golf course and was sitting on a hay bale fanning herself with her pink bridesmaid's hat. Bits of frizzy hair stuck to her forehead.

Mrs. Potter slipped off her pink shoes and plopped down next to her. "I think even the baby is having fun." She patted her stomach. "He's kicking in time to the music."

"You want to dance some more?" Bridget asked Willow.

"I'd rather have another piece of cake."

Aunt Dawsie stopped waving good-bye to some kids in the back of a pick-up truck and drifted toward them across the grass.

"I've never had such a time," she said, "but I guess Early and I should think about leaving."

"I guess," Mrs. Potter said. "It looks like the boys have finished loading the last of your stuff."

Bridget saw her father and Earl near Cabin 13 closing the back of the vending-machine refill truck. She felt as if a hole had suddenly opened in the pit of her stomach.

"I still have to throw my bouquet," Aunt Dawsie said. "Over to my cabin, everybody."

Bridget stood in the crowd at the foot of the

porch steps. Aunt Dawsie turned her back and flung the bouquet over her shoulder. David jumped in front of Zella and snared it.

"Way to go!" shouted Danny.

"Good catch," said Aunt Dawsie. "It means you're the next to get hitched."

"Yikes!" David tossed the flowers over Bridget's head to Luke.

"Not me," Luke said and threw the bouquet up again.

Zella lunged for it. "Does it still count?" she panted. "Even if it's been passed around?"

Something on the porch pinged.

"Aunt Dawsie," Bridget said. "Don't you want to take your wind chimes?"

"Good heck, I forgot." Aunt Dawsie came down the steps and gave Bridget a hug. "What would I do without you?"

"All set, li'l darlin'?" Earl asked.

"Not quite," Aunt Dawsie told him. "Have you locked the door?"

Earl grinned. "You betcha. Tight as a drum."

"Then give me Bridget's present." Aunt Dawsie's white dress billowed around her as she bent down.

She placed a key in Bridget's hand and closed her fingers on it. "Now it's all yours."

"What's mine?"

"Your very own room," Aunt Dawsie said. "From me to you. Cabin 13."

BELMONT UNIVERSITY LIBRARY

CHAPTER
10

A WEEK LATER Bridget propped her sign against the wall of Cabin 13.

"It's hard to work the key," she said to Willow. "You have to push it in and wiggle it around."

The cabin still smelled faintly of pine needles and popcorn, but all the framed photographs near the stove and the rug with the deer on it were gone.

"It's the same," Bridget said, "but different."

They stood together by the door.

"I don't believe this," Willow said finally.

"Aunt Dawsie wrote her new number on that little pad by the telephone, and she left the television, because Earl has one, and even the jigsaw puzzle," Bridget explained.

"What are those things on the coffee table?" Willow asked.

"My free weights. She sent them in the mail. And come look in the kitchen."

She showed Willow the teapot and the painted tin box full of tea bags and the old electric popcorn maker.

"And there's popcorn and peanut butter and cold cereal and crackers in this cupboard," Willow said, opening doors. "And look, she's even left plates and cups—"

"And forks and spoons and all sorts of stuff in the drawers," Bridget told her, "and, oh, I didn't see these, little salt and pepper shakers! And there's more. Open the refrigerator."

"Oh, my gosh! Earl's packed the whole thing with sodas."

Bridget set the little salt and pepper shakers on the counter and stepped back to look at them. Willow spun around on one of the stools. The afternoon sun glowed through the jars of red thimbleberry jam.

"You want to see the bedroom?"

The bedroom closet was empty except for

Bridget's maid-of-honor dress, but there were tons of other hangers and extra pillows and blankets on the shelf.

"The blankets are for when it gets cold," Bridget said.

She flopped onto one of the beds. Willow sat on the other. "This is going to be a great sleepover. I'm glad you invited me."

"And that little table over there is perfect for homework. I can see most of the herons' tree through the window and the sun going down," Bridget added.

"You must be the only kid in the whole country to own a whole cabin," Willow said.

"I have to keep it clean myself. Mom says the new person helping out when we're in school has enough to do. And Dad says I have to eat suppers at home, even if I spend the night here, but I can rent it whenever I want and earn my own money. And I don't have to wait until I'm twelve."

"That's a lot better than working at the golf course anyway."

"So I was wondering about a bankbook," Bridget said. "I mean, how to get one."

"It's easy. You just go to the bank and ask, but you have to bring an adult."

They were quiet for awhile.

"I can't wait for supper to be over," Bridget said, "so we can come back here and see it with the lights on. And then we can get into our pajamas and I'll show you how to use the free weights maybe or we can make popcorn and watch TV if you want."

"Or sit out on your porch and do nothing and pretend I live here all the time."

"I was wondering," Bridget said after a moment. "Do you know how to knit?"

"Sure. I made a scarf once."

"Then I'm going to finish the hat," Bridget said, "and add a pom-pom and earflaps and give it to Aunt Dawsie as a surprise." She sat up and swung her legs over the side of the bed.

"But now I want to put up my sign. Right in the middle of the front door."

Willow held it in place while Bridget hammered in the nails.

"I made up the name myself," Bridget said.

They went down the porch steps to see how it looked from far away.

THE HERON'S NEST, the sign read. PRIVATE! PLEASE KNOCK!

In the distance, Bridget could hear the murmur of the river running. I have to remember to call Aunt Dawsie, she thought, and ask her to come to the bank with me after school on Monday.

"What do you want to do now?" asked Willow.

"Let's go inside," Bridget said, "and wait for someone to knock."

BELMONT UNIVERSITY LIBRARY
1900 BELMONT BLVD.
NASHVILLE, TN 37212-3757

74

BELMONT UNIVERSITY LIBRARY

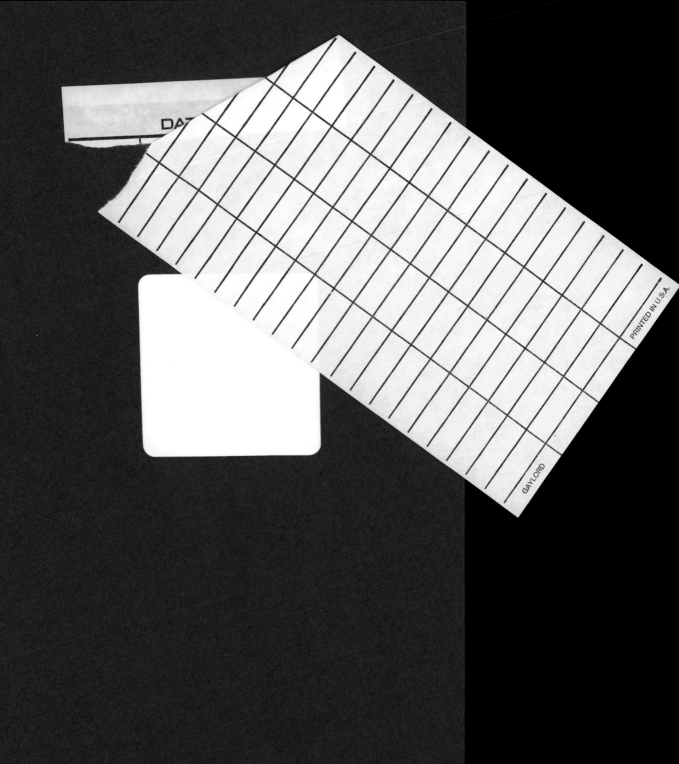

DATE

GAYLORD

PRINTED IN U.S.A.